For Eleanor Hubbard White

Hazel's mother gave Hazel a silver sixpence and a kiss and said, "Buy something nice for our picnic."

"I will," said Hazel, and she wheeled Eleanor's pram down the street.

Hazel stopped to help the postman.

"I see Eleanor has new shoes," said the postman.

"My mother made them," said Hazel. Eleanor's shoes were sky-blue silk.

"Good morning!" said the policeman. "I see Eleanor has
a new dress."

"My mother made it," said Hazel. Eleanor's dress was
calico with French lace trim.

"Such a pretty doll," said the baker.
"My mother made her," said Hazel.
The baker gave Hazel a buttercream rose.

Hazel bought two biscuits from the baker, one for herself
and one for Eleanor, but since Eleanor couldn't open
her mouth, Hazel ate them both.

With her last pennies she bought some grapes from the fruit
lady and a piece of bread with jam from the sandwich man.

"Can you find your way home, little girl?" asked the
fruit lady.

"Oh, yes," answered Hazel.

But at the next corner Hazel made a wrong turn.

After that she took another wrong turn and another,

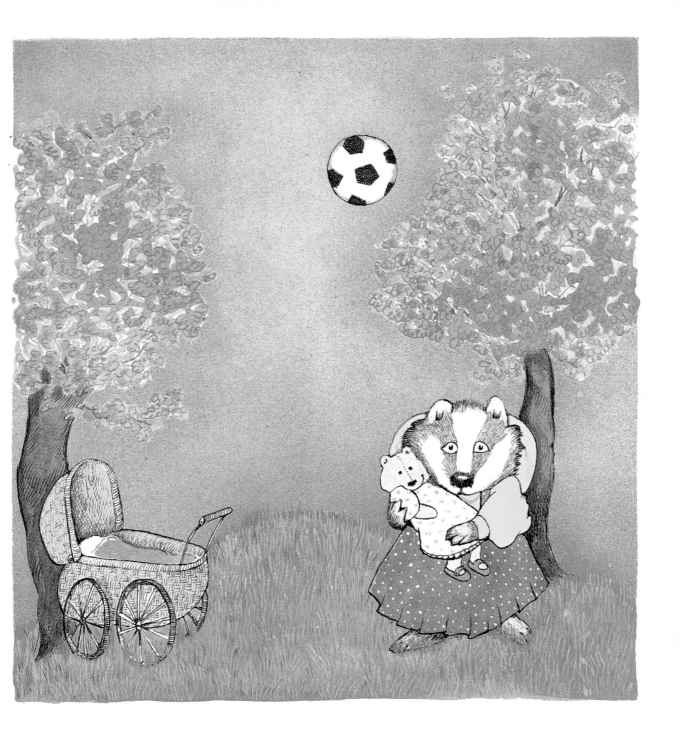

until she found herself on a lonely hilltop in a part
of town where she had never been before.

"Don't worry Eleanor," said Hazel, "We'll find our way back."

Just then a boy's voice rang out, "Hey, Doris! Someone's stealing our ball!"

In a flash Hazel was surrounded.

"What should we do, Doris?" asked the other boy.

"If she's going to play with our ball," said Doris, "we'll play with her doll."

Eleanor was tossed from hand to hand. Off came her
blue silk shoes.

"Stop!" Hazel shouted.

Higher and farther they threw her. Off came her calico dress.
Out came her stuffing.

"No!" pleaded Hazel. But she was powerless to stop them.

When they had finished with her, Eleanor was little more
than a rag.

"Eleanor, my Eleanor," said Hazel.

"Let's have a ride down the hill," said Doris.

Hazel rocked poor ruined Eleanor in her arms. She heard the pram splash into the pond at the bottom of the hill.

"Oh, Mother," she cried, "Mother, I need you!"

At just that moment, on the other side of town, Hazel's mother was picking the tomatoes for their picnic. Something told her Hazel needed her. A drop of rain fell. Then it began to pour and a great wind sprang up.

It blew the picnic blanket over the garden wall.
Hazel's mother caught hold of it but the wind was so strong

that it swept the blanket, Hazel's mother, the picnic basket, and a dozen tomatoes over the treetops as if they were no heavier than the blowing leaves.

The blanket filled with air, ballooned out, and sailed
over the town.

At last it lodged in the very tree where Hazel was sheltered from the rain. Doris and the boys were about to run home when Hazel's mother's voice boomed out from overhead, "Wait just a minute!"

A tomato hit Doris smack between the eyes.

"Don't make a move without fixing Eleanor!" Hazel's mother roared.

"Who are you?" Doris squealed.

"It's my mother!" said Hazel.

"Find Eleanor's dress and shoes!" rumbled Hazel's mother.
"Restuff her and sew her up as good as new!"
   Hazel's mother tossed her pocket sewing kit down to Doris.
It was followed by three more tomatoes.

The boys quivered like lemon jelly. "It was all Doris's fault," they yelled.

Hazel's mother laughed thunderously. "Fish that pram out of the pond and clean it up," she told them.

The boys scrubbed feverishly.
   Doris sewed like a machine.
   Above them the sun came out and the clouds slipped away.

Eleanor's pram worked without a squeak.

Eleanor was perfect except for her eyes, which Doris could not find in the grass.

The moment Doris and the boys left, Hazel's mother dropped to the ground.

Hazel's mother found the eyes and sewed them back on while Hazel ate a sandwich.

"Oh, Mother," said Hazel, "how did you do it?"
  "It must have been the power of love," said Hazel's mother.

Then they packed up and went home.

Hazel took two custard creams, one for herself and one for Eleanor, but since Eleanor couldn't open her mouth, Hazel ate them both.